Wrinkly Brinkly

Wrinkly Brinkly

by Jim Ertel

"Grandpa Jimmy"

Paladin Publishers

Wrinkly Brinkly
ISBN 978-0-9897387-4-3
Copyright © 2019 by James Ertel aka "Grandpa Jimmy"
P.O. Box 2111
Monument, CO 80132

Paladin Publishers
PO Box 700515
Tulsa, OK 74170

Represented by PriorityPR Group & Literary Agency.
www.prioritypr.org
Text Design/Layout: Lisa Simpson
Art by David Wilson

Acknowledgements

My beautiful wife of 50 years, Shirley. She is the love of my life and best friend. Willing to share the truth about my writing, but always with a helping of love on the side. An excellent proofer and editor.

Karen Hardin, owner of PriorityPR Group and Literary Agency, the best of literary agents. It would be hard to put a price on the value of her advice and expertise. She always goes above and beyond.

Mr. Sketches (aka David Wilson) artist extraordinaire. How he captures the look and emotion of a character on paper after a brief phone conversation is beyond me. He brought the characters of Wrinkly Brinkly to life, exceeding all my expectations.

A big thank you to Ty, my youngest grandson. He's an avid reader and first to read this book. He wrote a very thorough critique before knowing his Grandpa was the author. I took his comments seriously.

Thanks to Kate, my only granddaughter for reading as I wrote. She had many great suggestions.

Contents

Chapter 1

Run for Your Life

A mid-summer evening seldom passes without an elder inviting the kits to his lodge for a story. Lazy yawns and heavy eye lids soon follow, but every now and then a story is so exciting, so captivating that sleep is not possible. This was one of those nights, it was a story about the Black Ghost.

Bump never tired of hearing frightening stories of encounters with the Black Ghost. The scarier the better and the more he heard the more determined he was to find this extraordinary creature. Few had ever seen the illusive beast up close. And, except for one, those who may have, never returned to tell the tale. His beautiful black coat naturally concealed him in the shadows of the forest while his piercing blue eyes defied the darkness of night; a perfect combination for the ambush of unwary prey. It was said, he was so powerful and ruthless that even the mountain lion avoided him. And it was believed that his heart was made of stone, void of all mercy, kindness, or love; filled only with hate and a lust for blood. A wolf for sure, but unlike any other before him.

The elders had warned the kits to stay close to the water for the dark forest hides many dangers. To Bump, their words of warning seemed more like those of pirates trying to protect a hidden treasure. And on this evening, the story was so thrilling that it pushed him over the edge. His imagination went wild, like a roaring fire driven by powerful winds.

Bump wouldn't or couldn't wait another day. Bound and determined to discover the secret lair of the Black Ghost, that night he hastily devised a sketchy plan. Willow was the only one he would trust with the details and he planned to take her with him on this dangerous journey.

Bump and Willow were kits. Were they Labrador Retrievers instead of beavers, people would say they were full-grown but still puppies at heart. Old enough to care for themselves, exploding with unlimited energy, but lacking in cautious restraint and good judgement. They were only three years old in people years; that's twelve or thirteen in beaver years.

Willow was as graceful as a female deer. When she spoke, Bump's heart was aflutter. He thought she sounded like an angel; her voice as soft and gentle as a light breeze blowing through the trees. Bump on the other hand, could be heard coming from one end of the pond to the other. Everyone considered him to be quite obnoxious and he was usually in more trouble than all his brothers, sisters, and cousins lumped together. Yet, Willow was somehow able to see through it all. Underneath Bump's boastings, wild imaginations and impulsive quest for adventure beat the kind and gentle heart of her best friend.

His real name wasn't Bump, of course. Willow lovingly called him that because he was so preoccupied with thoughts of daring conquests that he seldom paid attention to where he was walking. Well, the nickname stuck, and it wasn't long before everyone called him Bump.

"Willow, this is what we'll do," said Bump. "We'll sneak away just before daylight. Then stay in the shadows of the rocks and trees where we won't be seen. Most important, we'll be very quiet. Everyone knows the Black Ghost prowls at night, so by morning he'll be sound asleep. He won't even know we're there," he assured Willow.

Early the next morning, Bump and Willow slipped away before the other beavers awoke. Bump was right about one thing, their dark fur coats made them seem to disappear as they moved through the shadowy forest. Willow tried to walk without breaking the smallest twig or rustling a single leaf.

"Bump," Willow said, "I thought we were supposed to be quiet."

"We are."

"Well, at least one of us is," she whispered. "You're making more noise than a bull moose galloping through the forest. We're getting a long way from the pond. . . Maybe we should turn back."

"It's okay, don't be scared Willow, I'll protect you. Come on, just a little further."

Far too far from the safety of the colony they stopped and hid behind a downed moss-covered pine tree at the edge of a meadow. They huddled there for a few moments staring at each other. Willow gripped bump's paw and held on tight. Then, in perfect unison, they took a deep breath, braced themselves on their webbed feet with their broad tails, and slowly raised their heads, just high enough to peer over the top. The meadow was inviting, it looked like the perfect playground for a kit, covered by a carpet of wispy green grass and arrayed with brightly colored spring flowers. Both instinctively knew that playground was reserved for the fast of foot. If threatened, deer and elk could sprint for the forest, but a slow-moving beaver wouldn't stand a chance. Across the meadow, just beyond the tree line was a granite cliff with a waterfall cascading down into a billowing mist at the bottom. Bump was fixated on that cliff.

"Willow, can you see that?" Bump whispered.

"See what?"

"There's a cave near that waterfall. Can't you see it? I'll bet it's the den of the Black Ghost."

"It's just a shadow Bump. We need to go back," she said, tugging at his leg.

Bump wasn't listening, "Come on," he instructed, leading Willow around the edges of the meadow closer to what he was sure was a cave.

Willow finally had enough of this foolishness, she stopped. "Bump, I'm not taking another step. Let's go home."

"Okay, we will, but wait here for a few minutes. I'll be right back, I promise. You'll be safe here."

Willow reluctantly released her death grip from Bump's paw. Bump moved forward alone, seemingly unaware that he had placed them both in grave danger. His imagination had escaped the boundaries of any common sense, wild with heroic thoughts of finding the secret lair. This time he walked quietly, at a turtle's pace, careful to place each paw in a spot that would avoid snapping the smallest twig. He inched his way around the edge of the meadow until he was close enough to see. There it was, a cave, hidden beneath a huge boulder. The trail leading to the entrance was worn, rutted and dusty, without grass or weeds. No doubt, something called this home. Any predator living in this cave had a clear view of the entire valley and the animals that grazed in the meadow.

This must be the lair of the Black Ghost, he thought. He dropped to his belly crawling even closer for a peek. As he neared the cave, he thought he heard something. Cautiously, he stood to his back feet and listened intently. There it was again, a creepy muffled sound coming from somewhere behind him. The fur on the back of his neck stood straight up. He turned his head to hear more clearly. This time, the sound was more like a deep snorting growl in perfect rhythm with the heavy breathing of what had to be a powerful animal. Even from his tip toes, with eyes as big as saucers, all he could see was thick spring grass. But like a ripple moving across a pond toward shore, the grass revealed the direction the creature was headed. Whatever was there, it was coming straight down the hill for the cave. Slowly at first, then faster and faster it came! In an instant, the thrill of discovering the lair evaporated. Bump was frozen in his tracks. His legs and feet felt like they had turned into giant stones of granite. His heart began to beat so hard it felt like it would burst, and his tongue was stuck to the roof of his suddenly dry mouth.

His mind raced, *don't just stand there; you've got to do something, Willow's in danger.*

The thought of Willow being hurt or worse forced him to break free of his paralyzing fear.

"Willow," he yelled, "He's coming, he's coming, run for your life!"

"Who?"

"The Black Ghost! Run Willow!"

Willow leapt from her hiding spot and sprinted in a straight line toward the trees on the other side. It was dangerous to cross an open meadow in the daylight, but they were running for their lives and that was the shortest way back to the colony. She was faster than Bump, reaching the tree line across the valley ahead of him. She stopped and looked back.

"Run faster, Bump," she yelled.

Willow turned and took off again with Bump close behind. They leapt from rock to rock, dodged pine trees, dove through the thick underbrush and jumped over downed timber. They had never run with such reckless abandon in all their lives.

"Just a little further Bump, we're almost there."

"Okay, I . . ..." THUD."

Willow turned to look, "Bump, get up, there's the pond."

"I'm right behind you Willow," he hollered as he tripped again tumbling head over heels down the steep hill.

"Jump!"

Willow made one last desperate leap, diving into the water. Bump ended his wild tumble with a comical, but painful belly flop on the water. Both swam straight to the bottom of the pond. Safe in their quiet underwater world of winding trenches and valleys, they navigated their way to the entrance of Willow's family lodge. They climbed inside where both took a deep breath and collapsed in exhaustion.

"Are you okay?" Willow gasped, trying to catch her breath.

"Yep, I'm fine, not a scratch," said Bump as he rubbed his very sore belly, "Are you okay?"

"Yes, but I was really scared Bump," she whispered, tears streaming down her cheeks. "I told you we should never have gone that far into the woods."

"She's right, you shouldn't have," came the words of a familiar gravelly voice behind them.

This was not part of the secret plan. Bump was sure that when they returned to the pond the rest of the family would be working on the dam. No one would suspect they had ever been gone. It almost worked.

Slowly they stood to their feet and turned to see who was lurking in the darkness of the lodge.

"Who's there?" asked Bump, as if he didn't know.

"You know," said the one in the shadows.

"Yes, PaPa," said Bump.

"Haven't you been warned about venturing too far into the forest?"

"Yes, PaPa."

"Well then. . ., perhaps you'll learn a lesson from your little scare. There are dangers in the forest that you can't possibly imagine. And today your foolish adventure not only endangered you Bump, but Willow as well. . ."

"But PaPa Winky," Bump interrupted.

"Bump, I know it's hard, but try to be quiet and just listen."

"But PaPa," Bump exclaimed, "The Black Ghost was chasing us, I think I saw him."

Wrinkly was the oldest and wisest beaver in the colony. Everyone called him "Wrinkly," except the kits of course. They liked to call him PaPa Winky. Like a loving grandpa, he always winked at the end of a story.

Wrinkly couldn't hold it in, he smiled and chuckled.

"I was watching you from the roof of your lodge. The only one chasing you was Tiny Fox. And he wouldn't have known what to do if caught you."

Then, Wrinkly's smile changed to a frown. He moved within paws reach of the kits, then stood up on his large web feet while supporting his tired old bones with his broad tail. He wasn't laughing. He looked directly into Willow's eyes and then Bump's.

"Listen carefully," he said. "Be thankful you didn't attract the attention of the Black Ghost. No beaver escapes his chase."

"But PaPa," Bump blurted, "you did."

Wrinkly didn't answer; he just shook his head, took a deep breath and exhaled in frustration. He dropped down to all fours, walked slowly past them and slid quietly into the water.

"It's true Willow, it's really true, PaPa Winky did get away from the Black Ghost."

Willow nuzzled up close to Bump, resting her head on his shoulder, crocodile tears growing in the corner of her eyes.

"Maybe so, but that doesn't mean we would have. I was scared Bump."

Bump leaned his head against hers and hugged her tight with both paws, "I know Willow, I was too. I'm sorry."

Chapter 2

If Only I Could

Most summer days, Wrinkly woke up early, at least an hour before sunrise. When he was a kit, it took only seconds for him to leap from bed and dive to his underwater world of adventures. But now, the chase for adventure was gone. It had been replaced with the painful task of stretching his sore old muscles.

Once limbered up, he put on a smile and slowly climbed to the top of his sturdy lodge. It had been built like a fortress by the most skillful builders in the colony. Every branch used for building was chosen for its strength and flexibility. Then, they were masterfully entangled in such a way they couldn't be ripped apart. Mud mixed with grass was pounded into every gap with the beaver's broad and powerful tails. It dried nearly as hard as concrete. No predator, not even a bear would ever get to Wrinkly. To make it comfortable, more mud mixed with aspen leaves was added on top to cover the rough branches. That made for a fine roof and a perfectly beautiful place for Wrinkly's tiny homemade rocking chair.

Wrinkly's lodge was colony central. From the top of his lodge he could be seen through the cool morning mist rocking peacefully; waiting for the sun to slowly appear above the snow-covered mountain that humans call Pikes Peak. "I always see things more clearly in the quiet of the morning," he liked to say. He had carefully crafted a hobbit pipe from a dried-up willow branch. Since he never actually smoked it, it was kept in the small pocket of his tiny checkerboard vest. Whenever he was asked a question, which was often, he would pull the pipe from his pocket and hold it to one side of his mouth before answering. He was convinced it made him look more thoughtful and wise. Next to his rocking chair there was always a fresh supply of tender aspen bark for snacking. He was never sure who placed it there, but he was thankful for the kindness. Gathering food had become quite difficult for old Wrinkly.

"Good morning Wrinkly, how are you this fine morning?"

"Finer than frog's hair," he replied to Rupert the toad.

"May I join you on your lodge?"

"Why certainly Rupert, I have a comfortable lily pad just your size next to my chair."

"Looks like the sunrise will be especially beautiful today, don't you think, Wrinkly?"

"Yes, I do, but you know what Rupert? Just once I'd sure like to see what our valley looks like from the top of that mountain."

"It must be quite a sight, I'm sure," said Rupert.

"My friend Regal has described its beauty many times Rupert. And every time he does, it makes me want to see for myself even more."

Regal was the most majestic eagle in the forest and best friends with Wrinkly. They had a very special relationship that began many years earlier when he helped save Wrinkly's life. People call him a bald eagle, but he isn't bald at all. His head and neck are covered with cloud white feathers; a perfect contrast to black eyes set in yellow and a golden beak. When Wrinkly stood on his back feet, Regal was still twice as tall. His huge wings nearly spanned the width of the lodge and allowed him to soar high above the valley with scarcely a flap. He used his strong talons to swoop in low and snatch two-pound trout from the river for breakfast. Then, late in the morning, once his family had been well fed, he would glide in for a perfect landing next to Wrinkly. The two old friends would talk for hours.

"How does Regal see our valley?" croaked Rupert.

"Well, why don't we let him tell us? Here he comes."

With a couple of big flaps of his wings Regal landed softly and settled in next to Wrinkly.

"Good morning Regal."

"Good morning Wrinkly. Good morning Rupert," he replied.

"Regal, Rupert would like to know how you see our valley from high above."

"Well I'd be happy to tell him. Rupert, just before the sun rises over the mountain, the valley and all the lodges of the colony are hidden beneath a foggy mist. When the mist gives way to the warmth of the morning sun it reveals the true beauty of our home. The hillsides come alive with all the colors of the rainbow as the flowers open to receive the rays of sunlight.

Lavender, yellow, blues and reds create a tapestry of color that can only be appreciated from high above. Willows line the banks along a staircase of dams and ponds that the families in the colony have masterfully built. The water is so clear that I can spot my breakfast from high above the trees. And not far from the ponds, a gentle stream disappears over the edge of a cliff into a shallow pool of blue water below. A place that Wrinkly and I know very well.

From up there, it's clear to me that only the Spirit of the Forest could have created something so beautiful. I like the evenings best of all Rupert, when all the commotion of the day gives way to the calm and peacefulness of our forest. The sunrise and the sunset are certainly beautiful from the roof of this lodge, but I sure wish you could see them from my point of view."

"If only I could, if only I could," said Wrinkly.

"I'd like to see that too, said Rupert, but how could an old beaver like you and a tiny toad like me ever reach the top of that mountain?"

Sadly, no matter how hard he thought, even wise old Wrinkly could not figure a way to make it to the top of Pikes Peak. It was too far for a small old beaver to walk and streams for swimming were only found in the valley.

"For now, Rupert, its beauty will have to remain in the imagination of my dreams and the words of my friend, Regal."

Chapter 3

They Called Him Wrinkly

You see, when Wrinkly was a kit, he looked like he had been born with a hand-me-down fur coat that was three sizes too big. His family thought he looked cute at first and they were sure he would eventually fill it out; but he didn't. Full grown and standing on his tiptoes, he was a head shorter than the rest of the beavers his age. His fur coat; more wrinkled than ever. He was never able to keep up with the others when they raced across the pond. He always finished last. And when it came to the tender branches of the willow tree, he had to settle for what was left near the ground. With the wrinkles came the never-ending teasing. "Here comes Wrinkly Brinkly," they would say. After a while, they dropped his real name and just called him Wrinkly.

When Wrinkly could endure their teasing no longer, he would dive to the bottom of the pond, then swim to his secret underwater hiding place. He had hollowed out a cavern beneath an enormous granite boulder in the deepest part of the pond. It was just big enough for one very small beaver. The water was so murky and the vegetation so thick that beavers swimming close by could not see him; the perfect place for a runt of a wrinkled beaver to hide from the world and mope. He couldn't understand why the Spirit of the Forest would create a beaver like him. *Maybe I'm a mistake,* he thought. He stayed hidden until his lungs began to ache. Then he would swim from under the boulder and rise, unseen, for a breath of air, allowing only the tip of his nose to break the surface.

What began as an escape from the ridicule of bullies, became a game for Wrinkly. *How long can I stay down this time,* he would think. Most of the beavers could hold their breath for about 15 minutes. Wrinkly, however, had practiced so much that he could stay under water and out of sight for nearly twice that long. It was the only thing that he could do better than everyone else. And one day, that ability, combined with the constant feelings of worth-lessness, drove him to attempt something extremely dangerous. Something that would end in tragedy and heartbreak.

There was one beaver, however, that refused to tease or mock Wrinkly. Gavi was his only friend and he never seemed to notice or care that Brinkly was wrinkled and short. When the other beavers were making fun, Gavi was there to step in and defend Wrinkly.

"Leave my friend alone," he would say. "One of these days you'll all wish to be his friend, you'll see."

Gavi could fell a tree in half the time it took the others. And he was able to solve the most difficult problems when building a dam in a rapidly moving stream. As hard as they may try, no one could out-swim him to the far side of the pond. When work needed to be done or a family needed help, Gavi was the first to arrive. And when a friend was in trouble, he came to their rescue just as he had often done for Wrinkly. The only thing Gavi seemed to need was the joy he felt when helping others. Wrinkly, like every other beaver, expected that Gavi would eventually become the leader of the colony.

Wrinkly spent most of his time alone. During the day, he stayed far away from the other beavers, working and playing by himself. Aside from Gavi, he felt like his only friends were frogs, turtles, and squirrels. They didn't seem to mind that he was wrinkled either.

The nights were worst of all. Loneliness would overwhelm him like a cold thick fog rolls in at evening. He would curl up like a ball in the darkest corner of his lodge. Then, he would cover his eyes with his paws and pray that sleep would come quickly. When he finally drifted off, Wrinkly entered a world of his own making. His imagination came alive, taking flight in the limitless universe of dreams. He imagined himself not as he really was, a small wrinkled beaver afraid of his own shadow, but as a super beaver, the guardian and protector of the colony. So real were these dreams that he began to believe they might come true. In that world he was never teased, never afraid and never felt alone.

"One day, when I'm older," he would tell Gavi, "I'll be the bravest beaver ever. I'll protect our pond and fight the enemies who try to destroy our colony. I'll show them," he would boast.

"Wrinkly," Gavi would answer, "You don't have to prove anything, you're fine just the way you are. You're quite special when you think about it. No one in the entire colony has a wrinkled coat like yours. And you know what? I think the Spirit of the Forest created you that way for an extraordinary purpose."

"Oh yeah? Tell me Gavi, how's the Spirit of the Forest going to use a little beaver with a wrinkled fur coat who can't swim any faster than a muskrat? If He's going to use anyone, it'll be you Gavi."

"I don't know about that, but I know He has a plan for your life and one day it will be revealed."

Gavi was right, Wrinkly did learn of his destiny, but it came at a cost that nearly destroyed him. He was the cause of a heartbreaking tragedy so awful that he became the most hated beaver in the colony. Not a single creature would have cared if he had simply wandered into the forest, never to return. And his story may have ended just that way, were it not for one very special visitor.

Today, Wrinkly is the leader of his colony and by far the oldest. A day never passes that he does not think about that tragic day and the visitor that changed his life forever. Yet, he has never spoken of either, or his incredible journey on the winding

Chapter 4

Promised to Tell

When the sun sets, animals of all kinds cautiously emerge from the forest for a cool drink and conversation with their friend, Wrinkly. The first to arrive along the ponds edge are does and fawns. Next, the cow elk and calves wander in followed by the bulls. The bucks and the bulls always stay behind, making sure no predators are trailing their families. Every now and then a member of the giant moose family visits too. Black, grey and brown squirrels, shy chipmunks, prickly porcupines, cuddly marmots and a few smelly skunks join the cast of characters before dark. Last of all, Regal arrives with a graceful landing on the branch next to his nest. It's atop a towering, carefully selected pine tree; with the perfect view of colony activities. Best of all, it's close enough to hear the questions asked of Wrinkly and the wisdom of his answers.

Every beaver in the colony and most of the forest animals listen intently to his every word. Even those who were once his enemy now believe in him. They trust his advice and most importantly, they are convinced that he possesses a supernatural power. Seldom does the night slip away without Wrinkly hearing the question, "When will you tell us your story Wrinkly?" Everyone is certain that hidden within that story is the truth of his encounter with the Black Ghost and the secret to his supernatural power. If no one asks, he can always count on Bump to remind him.

"PaPa Winky, you promised you would tell, you promised."

Wrinkly always responded in the same way. He would lean back in his chair, place his pipe in the corner of his mouth, and smile. "I know I promised and I will. . . when the time is right," he would say, "For now, be patient and remember this; when things go wrong the darkest day of your life may just turn out to be the beginning of something amazing."

But this evening his answer was a little different and it didn't go unnoticed.

"PaPa Winky, you didn't say it," blurted Bump.

"Say what?"

"You didn't say, 'when the time is right.' You always say you'll tell the story when the time is right."

"You're right Bump, I didn't. . . I've been giving this a lot of thought. You all know I'm getting old and I may not be around much longer. . ."

"Why, where ya goin' PaPa, I want to go with you." Bump interrupted.

"Bump," Wrinkly said.

"I'm sorry PaPa," Bump lowered his head and covered his eyes with his front paws.

Wrinkly continued, "The Spirit of the Forest has shown me the time is right. I have decided to tell my story on the evening of the next full moon."

Instantly, the hoot of the owl, the croaking of the frogs and the creaking of the crickets stopped. The gentle wind that was blowing ceased and the surface of the water became glassy smooth. The only sound was the gentle trickle of water streaming over the dam. Animals stood motionless, staring at one another in disbelief. Even Regal could hardly believe his ears.

With that, Wrinkly stood to his feet, "Good night everyone." Then, he turned, slipped into the water and slowly made his way to the underwater entrance of his lodge.

"Willow, PaPa's going to tell us the story of the Black Ghost, I can hardly wait."

Chapter 5

Alone and Afraid

His story really began when he was a kit. Unlike the deer or elk, Wrinkly was never able to count on speed or strength to escape the attack of a predator. If he had any hope of venturing beyond the confines of the colony pond and surviving, he would have to find a way to outsmart their enemies. He decided that the best way to do that was to learn their secrets. He was certain that if he understood the craftiness of the bobcat, the cunning of the wolf and the habits of the bears and mountain lions that he could find a way to outwit them. It was all part of the grand scheme he imagined in the world of his dreams. In that world, bright always prevailed over might.

To learn their habits, Wrinkly devised a plan to secretly observe the hunters. He started by venturing a little farther from the pond each day in search of hiding places near animal trails. When he found one that felt safe, he would hide there all night hoping to spy on a predator without being discovered. For days, weeks, and months the routine continued. In time, Wrinkly learned the habits of the most dangerous hunters in the forest. *Knowing this will give me the advantage,* he thought.

No one cared what Wrinkly was doing or what he thought. He only told Gavi and a few others what he was planning. Gavi listened but never encouraged him in his foolishness. The other beavers were not so wise. To them, his plans were crazy and yet so intriguing that they couldn't wait to tell their friends and then goad him into attempting one. Wrinkly became the center of attention as he described in detail how he would thwart these wily creatures. For the first time in his life he felt important. But with all his boastful words, he had failed to realize that he was backing himself into a dangerous corner. He would have to do more than talk or be completely humiliated, and, of course, endure the teasing that always followed. "You're all talk, Wrinkly," they would say, and then walk away laughing.

The truth was, when it came time to execute one of his plans, it made him sick to his stomach. Despite the nauseating fear, Wrinkly began taking dangerous chances to prove his clever ideas would work. They began small, but with each successful adventure his confidence grew. He soon discovered that the greater the risk he was willing to take, the more the other beavers seemed to admire him. He was hooked. It felt good to be accepted and praised instead of teased. The thrill of outwitting the slyest creatures of the forest was blinding his judgment and overpowering his instinctive fear.

The truth be known, the stories of his conquests were wildly exaggerated as they passed from one beaver to the next. Like the time he tricked a bobcat. From his secret hiding places, Wrinkly had observed that the bobcat always walked beneath the trunk of a fallen tree that spanned a dried-up river bed. It was part of his favorite hunting trail. One morning while it was still dark, Wrinkly watched as a human placed a wire box trap under the log and covered it with small branches and leaves. When the human left, Wrinkly investigated and found that the trap was big and strong enough to imprison a bobcat. This was his chance.

Early that evening, Wrinkly positioned himself near one end of the downed log. It was the time of day the cat began his hunt. When he was sure the bobcat was watching, he limped across the tree trunk holding one of his front paws close to his body as if it was injured. A defenseless little beaver would be an easy catch and a nice supper. He was certain the cat would be over confident and drop his guard. But it was risky; what if the cat failed to trigger the trap? Wrinkly felt like throwing up but choked it back.

The cat exposed his position early and charged at full speed. Wrinkly jump from the log and darted underneath, narrowly avoiding the trap. The cat, in hot pursuit, expecting to pounce on a frightened beaver, ran headlong into the cage. He went into a rage, struggling with all his might in a hopeless attempt to free himself. Hours later, when the noise of the struggle finally subsided, Wrinkly returned to the cage. The exhausted and frightened bobcat was lying motionless, mouth and lips bleeding, his paws rubbed raw. Wrinkly stared at the defenseless animal, *I'm even smarter than a bobcat,* he thought. Then he grinned and ran off, like a kid who had just absconded with grandma's cookie jar. As for the fate of the bobcat; he would soon be on his way to the zoo.

By the time the story had been told and retold in the colony, the 40-pound bobcat had mysteriously become a 150-pound mountain lion. And Wrinkly never corrected the story. He mistakenly believed this was all part of what Gavi had predicted. Those who had once made fun of him now seemed to be his friend.

"Wrinkly," they would say, "You're the bravest beaver in the colony. You could outsmart any animal in the forest." Their flattery felt good; never once did he consider the possibility that they were manipulating him. From that moment on the Ghost became an obsession. And by now, he had long forgotten the words of the elders. "Pride always comes before the fall."

The day finally came, when Wrinkly attempted to outwit the most cunning and feared animal in the forest. He was convinced this would be the greatest day of his life. "I'll be the most respected beaver in the colony," Wrinkly told Gavi, "no one will ever forget this day, and they'll all have to start calling me Brinkly," he boasted.

Gavi warned him, "Quit listening to the other beavers Wrinkly, you're about to meet an enemy you can't outsmart."

Wrinkly and Gavi were both right. No one ever forgot the day that Wrinkly came face to face with the Black Ghost. It didn't end well for Wrinkly or the colony. The huge bubble of pride that had been driving him burst. The praise of the colony turned to cruel anger and Wrinkly's hope for glory was replaced with the painful consequence of his actions. He did what he had always done; he retreated to the self-imposed solitary confinement of his lodge. Alone and afraid, he cried himself to sleep. There were no longer fanciful dreams to easy his pain, only nightmares. Not a single member of the colony ever came to comfort him. That day would always be remembered, but in a way that Wrinkly could never have imagined.

And now, the time had come. Wrinkly was ready to tell his story.

Chapter 6

Full Moon

Bump and Willow were the first to arrive and claim their seats. The best ones, of course, were atop PaPa Winky's lodge at the foot of his rocking chair. Other friends arrived early too and found their place near the pond's edge. Soon, the growing hum of whispers sounded like that of a beehive during the peak of pollen season. If anticipation were honey, it would have been dripping from the honeycomb.

"Bump," Willow said, "I know it will be hard for you, but don't interrupt PaPa Winky tonight. Promise me."

"Okay, I promise," he said rather reluctantly.

The sky was crystal clear and the air crispy cold; a perfectly comfortable night for furry friends. The full moon glowed so brightly that it made you feel like you could reach up and touch it. The reflection of twinkling stars off the glassy water made the whole valley sparkle like frost covered trees in the early morning sunlight. It was as though the Spirit of the Forest had set the stage Himself.

The whispers ceased, and all eyes focused on Wrinkly as he climbed atop his lodge. He sat down, leaned back in his rocking chair and placed his pipe in the corner of his mouth. He rocked quietly for a few moments, scanning his now silent audience; then smiled. "Well, where shall I begin?"

"Tell us how you escaped from the Black Ghost," Bump blurted.

Wrinkly looked down at Bump with one of those, PaPa Winky, be quiet looks.

Willow covered Bump's mouth with her paw, "Let PaPa tell the story," she whispered.

"Okay, I'm sorry," he mumbled.

Wrinkly continued, "I was about four and a half years old at the time, (that would be about age eighteen in people years). I had just completed what I thought was the grandest heroic plan ever. It would rid the colony of our most threatening adversary, the Black Ghost. It was dangerous, but I had convinced myself that it would work, despite the warnings from my best friend, Gavi."

Bump was sitting at attention, ears and eyes locked on Wrinkly. Then, PaPa Winky said, "The story really began long before that." Like air escaping a balloon, Bump let out a soulful sigh and dropped to his belly.

"My real name isn't Wrinkly," he said. "That was the nickname I was given by the other beavers when I was a kit, kind of like you, Bump. I love the name now, but hated it then. I hated being small. I hated my wrinkled fur coat and most of all I hated being teased.

Most days, I felt sad and lonely. All I wanted to do was run away and hide. Perhaps some of you have felt like that too. At night, I would curl up in a little ball in the darkest corner of my lodge, longing for sleep. When it finally overpowered my restless mind, the imagination of my dreams transported me into another world. In that world I was a super beaver; strong, brave and the heroic defender of the colony. I was always able to outsmart our dreaded enemies, and everyone loved me. I wanted to live there forever. But in the morning, I would awaken to a world that hadn't changed, at least for me. However, the dreams did serve one purpose; they filled my mind with extraordinary ideas. Maybe I really could outsmart our enemies. That's what I wanted to believe.

By the time I was old enough to be on my own, I had convinced myself it was true. If I succeeded, I would be considered the bravest beaver that had ever lived in the colony. The teasing would be replaced with cheers of admiration and the loneliness with love and acceptance. No more hiding.

To outsmart wily predators, I would first have to learn their habits. Every evening before leaving the safety of my lodge I rolled in the thick slime at the edge of the pond, coating my fur with mud. The dangerous predators I planned to watch all had a keen sense of smell. One whiff of my scent, and the end would come quickly. Once my scent was disguised, I would venture deep into the ghostly forest searching for the perfect hiding places. From hollowed out logs, thick tangled underbrush and tiny crevasses between boulders I studied the habits of the animals that hunt in the night. It was a risk that only a desperate and foolish beaver would take. The fox, bobcats, mountain lions and even bears strolled past unaware of my presence.

As it turns out, bears were the easiest of all to observe. They feel no need to be quiet and couldn't care less who sees them, except possibly humans. They have no natural enemies; no other animal would dare to challenge them. They're strong and powerful, yet no real threat to the colony, so long as we build our lodges correctly. I often wished I were a bear, then every animal in the forest would have to respect me. I liked to call them "kings of the mountains." I was certain that if the Spirit of the Forest were an animal, He would most certainly be a bear.

Mountain lions are deadly but hunt mostly for deer and elk and stay in the high country. They only come near the pond to drink at night when beavers are safe in their lodge. Wolves were the most difficult to observe. I seldom saw one, and then only at a distance. They hunted in packs, chasing their intended victim for hours, driving them to exhaustion. When their prey could run no more, it came to a bloody end.

I discovered that all predators are creatures of habit, hunting the same trails in the same way night after night. Except for the wolf, their habits were so predictable I was certain that I could set a trap for any one of them.

Once, I tricked a bobcat into getting caught in a trap that had been set by humans. The news of that encounter swept through the colony like wildfire. The next thing I knew, the young bobcat had somehow morphed into a full-grown mountain lion. I never bothered correcting the story. I had respect, or so I thought.

I wanted more. I was determined to prove I was clever and brave enough to be a leader in the colony. In my mind, the only way a wrinkled little beaver could do that was to destroy the most dangerous and elusive hunter of all. There was only on problem. I was beginning to believe that perhaps the Black Ghost was a ghost. I had never actually seen him. But I was sure I heard his sinister howl. It sounded more like a mocking laugh than a howl, with an unmistakable threatening tone that sent chills down my spine.

If he was more than a ghost, I would have to venture even farther into the forest to learn the truth. This time my hiding place would have to be the most well concealed of all. My plan would have to be imaginative, clever and daring. There was no room for error, this was not a predator that could be fooled by a simple trick.

A Great Discovery

Every beaver in the colony knows that our pond is fed by an underground stream. We all know its source now, but we didn't back then. The elders warned us; don't attempt to swim the underground stream, some have tried and never returned. Those warnings only served to inspire a secret club among the young and adventurous, The Brotherhood of Heroic Beavers. Admission was simple. Defy the elders warning and swim the stream to find its source. When a beaver wanted to join, the members gathered near the edge of the pond where the stream bubbled up. The one making the attempt would take the deepest breath possible, dive to the underwater entrance and then swim as far up the stream as he could. He would turn around with just enough air left in his lungs to make it back. If he went too far, he could drown; there were no air pockets along the way to catch a second breath. Even if one existed, it was so dark in that swirling underground world it couldn't be seen. It seemed impossible.

When those in the club saw me coming, they laughed. "This is only for the fast and the strong Wrinkly," they would say.

I had never actually tried to swim the underground stream. Yet, I was probably the only one who had a chance of reaching the source. I could do something the rest of the beavers could not. When I was young and wanted to be alone, I retreated to my secret underwater hiding place. . . a hollowed-out cavern beneath a boulder in the murkiest and darkest part of the pond.

"And the answer is No, Bump, I won't show you where it is," Wrinkly said with a smile.

I would stay there until I felt like my lungs would burst, then rise to the surface, take another breath and head back down. It became a game for me. Eventually I learned to hold my breath nearly twice as long as the others. Surely that could make the difference.

I decided to try early one morning. There would be no audience for this attempt. I took a breath, dove to the entrance and began swimming. The stream twisted and turned in every direction as it flowed around jagged rocks and snaked through a maze of roots. The farther I swam the gloomier it became, until I was swimming in total darkness by feel. What little confidence I had, quickly turned to fear and then panic. My heart was racing, and my webbed feet felt like rubber. I turned around and swam with all my might. When I reached our pond, I darted for the surface, aching for a breath of air. With quivering legs, I struggled to crawl atop my lodge. When my mind cleared, I realized I had only been gone for a couple of minutes. It wasn't the swim that caused my heart to race and burn the oxygen in my lungs so quickly, it was fear. I would wait until I was fully recovered and then try again.

This time I would pace myself, taking it slow and easy. I dove to the entrance, then carefully but steadily made my way upstream. I was so practiced at holding my breath that I knew exactly when I had reached the point of no return. If I didn't head back then, I would most likely drown. I was about to turn around when a dim light appeared in the distance. Without thinking, I swam for it, hoping there would be a breathing hole at the surface. It turned out to be a small opening just big enough to get my head above ground. I took several deep breaths while clinging to roots that kept me from being pulled under by the current. Then I chewed away at the edges of the opening. When it was large enough, I squeezed through, pulling myself up and out.

I was in the middle of a lush green meadow and a very long way from the colony. It was beautiful but no place for a beaver in plain sight of predators. I slipped back into the stream, took another huge breath and headed farther upstream. I hadn't gone far when another light appeared. The closer I got the brighter the light and the wider the stream. Then, the force of the rushing water subsided. My heart began racing again; it was excitement this time, not fear. When I surfaced, I was in a beautiful clear pool well inside the tree line of the forest. My slow steady pace had paid off.

On the far side, a stream spilled over the edge of a high granite wall as a beautiful waterfall. The force of the falling water had created a deep pool at the base. From there it continued underground on its journey to our colony's pond. This was it, the source that no other beaver had been able to reach. I felt like swimming to the shore and dancing, but I knew better. My eyes and the end of my nose were the only parts above water. There was no telling who or what might be prowling nearby. The pond was teaming with fish, if I swam too quickly they would scatter, splashing the water like an alarm. I glided through the water without the smallest ripple until reaching the base of the falls.

I lifted my head high enough out of the water to survey the surroundings. What I saw sent chills through my body. I froze, floating motionless, afraid to breathe; both terrified and captivated by his presence. Sitting quietly at the entrance to a cave, a stones throw away, was the most beautiful black wolf I had ever seen. As if he knew I was watching, he turned his head and stared. It felt like his piercing blue eyes were looking right through me. Everything inside was screaming, *dive to the bottom, swim for your life,* but I couldn't look away from this magnificent creature. Then, he casually yawned, exposing his deadly fangs, licked his lips and vanished into the darkness of the cave. He had no idea I was there. I think that's when my heart began beating again.

It was time to go home. I sank beneath the water and swam to the opening where the water escaped into the darkness of the underground. The swim was much faster, the current pushing me along. There was no need for a stop at the breathing hole, but I couldn't resist one more peek. I climbed out and stood to my back feet, watching as the water spilled over the cliff into the mist of the pond. All seemed peaceful when a sudden shiver swept through me, I had the spookiest feeling that I was being watched. Back in the water I dove, my mind swirling like the current on my way home.

Discovering the source of the underground stream paled in comparison to finding the lair of the illusive Black Ghost. He wasn't a ghost at all and lived closer to our colony than anyone ever suspected. The impossible had just become possible. Surely, I could find a way to destroy him. When I reached my lodge, I immediately began planning his end.

Every day, I risked the treacherous swim to the pool. The reeds and willows were thickest at the edges near the falls. I felt safe there and it provided an unobstructed view of the cave. I soon learned that it was just before sunrise and right after sunset that the Black Ghost was most active. He was a creature of habit just like the other hunters. He left his lair late each evening and returned early every morning. When he returned he would sit near the entrance for a short while and then disappear into the dark cavern where I assumed he was sleeping. That assumption was my first mistake.

The Grand Plan

Just above the cave sat a precariously balanced gigantic boulder. It seemed to be the only thing preventing tons of loose rocks from sliding down the face of the cliff. Not far from the cave was one of the tallest pine trees in the forest. That gave me an idea! If I could cause that tree to fall directly on the boulder it might come crashing down bringing a mountain of rocks with it. That would seal the entrance to the cave forever. And if my timing was right, it would become the grave of the Black Ghost.

From early summer to mid fall, I continued to study the Black Ghost. Like all other predators, his habits never varied. I also practiced felling large pine trees near the edge of the colony pond. They were of no value to the colony for food and too large to use for the dam. When asked what I was doing, I'd answer, "Just wanted to see if I could fell these tall trees."

"What a waste," I was told. They had no idea I was learning to fell a tree in a very specific direction. And, exactly how much of the trunk could be gnawed away before it would crash to the ground. The only one who didn't think I was crazy was my only friend, Gavi.

"Wrinkly, I know you, you're up to something, what is it?" said Gavi.

"I'll tell you," I told Gavi, "but you have to promise not to say anything to anyone." He agreed. "I swam up the underground stream and found its source. It's a deep pool with a waterfall. That's where I discovered it."

"Discover what?" Gavi asked?

"The entrance to the Black Ghost's lair. He lives in a dark cave just a little way from that pool and I have a plan to entomb him in that cave forever."

Gavi was the strongest and bravest beaver of all, but now there was a look of fear on his face that I had never seen before. "Wrinkly, whatever you're planning, please, don't try it. The Black Ghost is smarter than you think; I'm afraid for you."

"Don't worry." I told Gavi, "I know what I'm doing."

Wrinkly stopped with his story and looked down at Bump, "Does that sound familiar Bump?" He asked.

"Yes PaPa."

Wrinkly continued. "Gavi, I've been watching the Black Ghost all summer and I'm ready to put my plan into action. In a few days, the Black Ghost will be gone and I'll be the hero, you'll see."

Gavi pleaded, "Wrinkly, you don't need to prove anything. It's too dangerous."

But it was too late. My mind was made up. After all, the only life at stake was mine. That assumption was my second mistake. I was about to learn the hard way that everything you do in life affects others. And all of you here tonight would do well to heed that warning. Right Bump"

"Yes PaPa."

The next evening, I went to work; swimming to the pool just before sunset where I floated quietly in the reeds until the Black Ghost was long gone. Convinced I was alone, as always, I rolled in the mud to cover my scent. Then crawled inch by inch on my belly to the base of the giant pine tree. Its trunk was much larger up close and would take longer to gnaw away than I had anticipated. I began chipping away on the side of the tree facing the cave; stopping every few chomps to look up and listen. It took three nights to chew a little over halfway through the trunk. If my calculations were right, the tree would fall toward the boulder above the cave.

On the fourth night, I began gnawing on the opposite side of the trunk. That was the tricky part. If I went too far, the tree would fall while the Ghost was away. If I didn't gnaw deep enough, then the last cut, the most dangerous cut of all, might be my last. That cut had to be done in the daylight after the Ghost had entered his cave. If it took too long, the Black Ghost would certainly awake, sealing my fate, not his.

I chose what I thought was going to be a stormy day, hoping the sounds of rain and thunder would help disguise the crackling of the tree as it fell. One last time I swam up upstream, arriving just before daylight. There I waited for the Black Ghost. Right on schedule he strolled up to the cave. He stopped, almost as if he was intentionally posing, the morning sun silhouetting him against the glittering granite wall. It made me wonder how a creature so beautiful and majestic could be so evil. He turned his head, peering at the pool through those steely blue eyes. It felt eerie. Could he hear my pounding heart? Did he know I was there? I waited, frozen in place among the reeds and cattails. Like a rattlesnake coiled to strike, I was ready to explode with a burst of speed propelling myself to the safety of the underground stream. One step in my direction and I was gone. Then, as he always had, he yawned and disappeared into the dark of his lair. The sky was clear now, there would be no disguising the noise of a falling tree.

I forced myself to swim to the edge of the pool and roll in the thick mud. Then, for some unexplainable reason I looked up. At the very top of the waterfall a sparkling white mist appeared. It was unlike anything I had ever seen. At the same time a wonderful smell of wild roses filled my nostrils. For a few rational seconds I considered abandoning the whole idea. But like a dark storm cloud shuts out the sunlight, my selfish pride quickly clouded that moment of clarity. That was my third and final mistake. I made myself crawl toward the tree, heart pounding and every muscle in my body trembling. It felt as if all the strength was draining from my body. I reached the tree and started gnawing, slowly at first then faster and faster. It seemed like an eternity before the giant tree revealed its intentions with pops and crackles. I glanced at the cave. No Black Ghost.

I backed away to watch as this giant tree gained momentum, headed directly for the boulder. It hit with the force of an earthquake; the earth shook beneath my feet. That was followed immediately by the deafening thunder of a rock slide. I dove for cover. When the ground quit shaking and the dust cleared, I cautiously moved from under an old tree trunk. I couldn't believe my eyes. The entrance to the cave was buried behind a mountain of rocks and boulders. The sound of the crash must have frightened every creature into running for their life. Not even a bird could be heard chirping. Again, I looked up. A familiar young eagle was soaring above. Below him that glowing white mist at the top of the falls had grown brighter and thicker. It now obscured the top of the granite wall where the stream began its plunge to the pool below. The eagle looked down and then quickly darted away at full speed in the direction of the colony.

I should have run for the safety of the pond right then, but I had to know for sure. One cautious step at a time I approached what moments before had been the entrance to his lair. When I reached the enormous pile, I stood to my back feet for a better look. Gradually, the fear that had nearly paralyzed me was being replaced with excitement. I started to laugh and then covered my mouth with my paw. It didn't help. The more I tried to hold it in, the louder it got until I was jumping with joy. I had done it; I had destroyed the Black Ghost. I couldn't wait a second longer! I had to tell Gavi and the colony about this awesome feat. I spun around, intending to sprint for the pond, then stopped dead in my tracks.

There he stood, like a mighty evil king about to pronounce judgment. His piercing blue eyes were filled with hate, the fur on his neck was standing straight up and ears were flattened against his head. I tried to back away, but I was trapped against the face of the cliff with nothing between me and the Black Ghost. He let out a low growl, exposing his sharp fangs as he slowly moved toward me.

"Stupid foolish little beaver," he growled, "Did you really think you could kill me?"

"But, but I saw you enter the cave," I stuttered.

"You thought you were so smart, spying on me every night. You saw what I wanted you to see. What you don't know is that my lair has a hidden passage on the back side of the mountain. While you thought I was sleeping, I was stalking your every move. I could have killed you the first night you dared enter my pond. But I decided to turn it into a game. Now that you've destroyed the entrance to my cave, I'm tired of that game. It's time to end it!"

I was about to die, yet thoughts and questions raced through my mind at lightning speed. How could I have been so foolish and prideful? Why hadn't I listened to the elders and my friend Gavi? Everything was so clear now, but it was too late. No one would know what happened; all they would remember was that a wrinkled little beaver had gone missing. Few would even care.

The Black Ghost moved in for the kill, one slow step at a time. I think he enjoyed watching his victim tremble in fear. He was so close I could feel his breath on my face. It smelled of dead flesh. He towered over me, mouth wide open, drawn lips exposing his deadly fangs. The saliva dripping from the corners of his mouth splatting on the rocks at my feet. Nowhere to run, I closed my eyes, surrendering to the inevitable, hoping the Ghost would end it quickly. Then, a kind of peace came over me and all fear evaporated. *Was this death*, I wondered? But before I could open my eyes, a shout pierced the silence.

"Run, Wrinkly, run."

I opened my eyes as the Black Ghost turned to see who was coming. It was Gavi, he was running full speed and headed directly for the Ghost.

"Run Wrinkly, get to the pond," Gavi shouted.

He leapt on the back of the surprised Black Ghost, sinking his long sharp teeth into the nape of his neck with all his might. I sprinted for the pond, dove in and swam for the underground stream. Then, the reality of what was happening hit me. I was suddenly terrified for my friend Gavi. I stopped swimming and rose cautiously to the surface. It was all over. The Black Ghost was straddled over the lifeless body of my friend. He looked straight at me then tilted his head back and released that sinister howl. It sent waves of fear through my body.

"Your time will come stupid little beaver. You'll soon join your friend."

That was the last time I saw Gavi or the Black Ghost.

Only Bump dared say a word. "PaPa, how did Gavi know you were in trouble?"

"It was my friend Regal. Gavi had asked him to watch out for me. When he saw the Ghost reappear on the back side of the cave after the rock slide, he knew I was in trouble. So, he immediately sped to tell Gavi. "

"So Gavi saved your life, PaPa."

"Yes, he did Bump. The strongest, smartest and most loved beaver in the colony gave his life for this foolish little beaver that everyone called Wrinkly. It was unforgivable. And if it were not for a special visitor, I believe I would have died from a broken heart."

Chapter 7

New Beginnings

After that terrible day, my life was never the same. Unwilling to face the colony, I stayed isolated in my lodge; except for a few short swims to my under-water pantry. The surface of the pond would soon freeze so the few willow branches I had taken time to store would have to last through the long frigid days of winter. During the lonely nights, I no longer imagined days filled with glory and conquest. I only hoped for a time when my broken heart would heal, and the colony would forgive me. Both seemed impossible. Little did I know that those dark days would become the key to unlocking a door of a new beginning. It was the beginning of a journey that led me down a path of amazing discovery, and what I discovered changed my life forever.

When I emerged from my lodge the following spring, I kept to myself; staying busy improving my lodge and helping repair breaches in the dam. The anger the colony had once felt for me seemed to have lessened. Now, they simply ignored me. Somehow that felt worse than being hated. The best thing to do was speak very little and help the colony. One way was to be vigilant, and then be first to sound the alarm when danger approached. A hard slap of a beaver's tail on the water let the others know that danger was near. When they heard that distinctive slap, they would run for the pond and dive to the safety of their lodge. Instead of joining them, I climbed to the top of the closest lodge. The sight of one wrinkled little beaver standing tall on his back feet and waving his paws wildly surprised even the fiercest of predators. It held their attention long enough to allow the others to escape. When all were safe, I lunged for the water. I wasn't trying to be brave, I was terrified. But I owed the colony a debt that could never be repaid. If I were killed, I was only getting what I deserved.

That fall, a very hungry bear, wanting to fatten up for winters hibernation, wandered near our pond. He realized that a break in our dam had allowed the water to drop dangerously low. As he approached to investigate, I slapped the water with my tail then climbed atop my lodge, waving my paws. This bear glanced at me with little interest. He was following his nose. He easily broke through the thin ice, then waded in the belly deep water to the largest lodge. His sense of smell told him this was a full house. It was the home of a family with half a dozen kits. They had all heeded the warning and were huddled together in their lodge. He began his rampage, ripping at the roof with his huge claws and teeth. I could hear the fearful squeals of the kits inside. If the roof didn't hold, the water was far too shallow for an escape. The entire family would be lost. After one failed attempt to break through, like most bears, he gave up in search of an easier meal.

He stood to his hind feet and looked in my direction. Once again, the unnerving eyes of a deadly predator were focused on me. He bounded from that lodge and charged. I dove for the safety of my lodge and waited. It wasn't long before I heard him climb on top where he attempted to rip through. Eventually he gave up on my lodge too. All hope for a beaver snack was gone. He growled in frustration one last time and then wandered off. When the attack was over, I laid down and closed my eyes. That was more than enough excitement for one day.

The Voice

I was nearly asleep when I heard the Voice. "I love you Brinkly," it said. I jumped to my feet, front paws spread wide, back straight and my nose pointing to the ceiling. I thought that made me look much bigger and fiercer. "Who's there?" I demanded. I spun around and around, examining every nook and cranny of my lodge. "Who's there," I repeated. But there was no answer nor an intruder to be found. I rubbed my eyes. *Was I dreaming?* Once calm, I took a deep breath and laid back down. That's when I noticed the smell of wild roses. I wasn't sure what to make of that, but those words, "I love you Brinkly," kept replaying in my mind. Sleep did not return.

Next morning, I joined the other beavers at sunrise to help repair the breach. By now, the colony had gradually gone from ignoring me to tolerating my presence. Now and then one would even bark an order. "Move that branch over here," he would demand. At least someone was talking to me, an improvement as far as I was concerned. All day I worked packing mud and grass into gaps between the branches. But my thoughts were not on the dam, all I could think about was that voice. I could hear the words, "I love you Brinkly," as clearly in my mind as I had in the darkness of the lodge. And no one had called me Brinkly for years. *It had to be real, but who had spoken those words?* I had to know. When the breach had been repaired, the dam was even stronger than before, nearly indestructible.

I returned to my lodge, half hoping for peaceful sleep and half hoping to hear the Voice. When I couldn't stay awake another minute, the Voice spoke to me again. "I love you Brinkly." This time I didn't move a muscle. His words were more than just words. They made me feel like warm oil was flowing over my entire body. It was unlike anything I had ever felt. My old friend Gavi had a voice that made me feel like he cared, but it was nothing like this. And besides, Gavi was gone. "Who are you," I asked.

"I'm the Spirit of the Forest, Brinkly, and I've come to help you."

That was when I realized that the visitor was not someone I could see with my eyes. He was more like an invisible loving presence. His voice seemed to be coming from everywhere, or perhaps from deep within my soul. It was hard to know. But His every word made me feel loved and accepted; something I hadn't felt for a very long time. The aroma of roses flooded my lodge. I said the only thing I could think of, "Please don't leave."

"Brinkly, I am the Spirit of the Forest, I've been watching over you all your life. I've never left you and I promise I never will. I love you."

Tears began to trickle down my cheeks. *Why would anyone love me after what I had done?* I thought to myself.

"Because I've forgiven you," said the Spirit of the Forest.

His response frightened me. I was certain I hadn't voiced a single word of that thought aloud.

"Don't be afraid Brinkly," the Spirit said, "I know your every thought, your strengths and your weaknesses. After all, I created you just the way you are, and I love you."

Those were the last words the Spirit of the Forest spoke that night, which was probably a good thing. My body was trembling, and my mind struggled to understand. I laid there trying to make sense of what just happened; wondering if He would return, hoping He would. Then, out of nowhere, the memory of Gavi's words flooded my mind. *"You're actually quite special when you think about it. No one in the whole colony has a wrinkled fur coat like yours. And you know what? I think the Spirit of the Forest created you this way for an extraordinary purpose."*

A few days later, He was waiting for me. The moment I entered my lodge I felt His presence and smelled the roses. I wasn't afraid. This all-powerful Spirit of the Forest, creator of everything, made me feel like I was in the presence of a friend.

"I know you're bursting with questions, Brinkly, so go ahead, ask. But keep in mind that some things are not for you to know."

Most of the time, I asked what must have seemed to Him like dumb questions, but He listened patiently. Then, He would answer like a loving father helping his kit understand. Or, He would repeat, "that's not for you to know." Every word He spoke felt like a healing ointment being applied to my broken heart. And much too soon for me, His visit was over. However, before leaving, the Spirit always took time to share a story about another beaver in the colony.

"Did you know that old Lester across the pond is having trouble repairing his lodge; seems he can't swim with those heavy branches anymore."

I understood. The Spirit was not just telling a story, He was asking me to help. Then, as He departed, He always repeated these words, "Tell no one of our conversations."

Early every morning I began the day by helping the beaver the Spirit had told me about. At first it was nothing more than a lot of work. But after a while, I grew to appreciate how good it felt. My friend Gavi had certainly understood that. Little by little, day by day, my life was becoming more about others and less about myself.

Chapter 8

Destiny

One night, I asked the Spirit of the Forest this question. "You said You came to help me. What did You mean?"

"I was wondering how long it would be before you asked. I've come for two reasons, Brinkly. The first and most important you already know. I came to be your friend. I'm the friend who is closer than a brother, the One who will never leave or forsake you, and I'm the healer of your broken heart. Being your friend is easy, but healing your heart, that's more difficult. It requires your cooperation."

"Whatever it is, I'll do it." I replied.

"When the time is right, I'll tell you what you must do. For now, trust me. My second reason for our visits will surprise you. I'm here to help you fulfill your destiny."

He was right, I had not imagined that. But instead of saying the first thing that came to mind, I thought for a minute. Thinking before speaking was one of the first lessons I learned from the Spirit.

"Did you hear what I just said, Bump?"

"Yes, PaPa."

So, after thinking about it Bump, I said to the Spirit, "I once dreamed of a life filled with excitement and adventure. In that world, I was brave and fearless, destined to lead. But when I attempted to make that happen, it ended in the death of my only friend. My only desire now is for the pain and heartache to go away."

"I understand Brinkly. When you're alone, thoughts of Gavi flood your mind. And when you sleep, every dream ends with the same nightmare; a haunting image of Black Ghost standing over Gavi's lifeless body. Don't let your heart be troubled or fearful any longer. I'm with you in those dreams. There is nothing you have done or will do that could separate you from My love. It's eternal and unconditional."

I can't express the feelings of love and compassion that flooded over me in that moment. I lowered my head as a flood of tears poured down my cheeks.

The Spirit continued, "In your heart, you believe that the rest of your life should be dedicated to making amends for Gavi's death. You see it as a huge debt that will never be fully repaid. And you believe you're getting exactly what you deserve. But that's not true Brinkly."

"It's not?"

"No. You could never pay a debt so great as the loss of Gavi. And you don't have to. . ."

The Spirit waited to let that sink in.

"Then why have you been encouraging me to work so hard for the colony," I said in frustration.

"I've been preparing you Brinkly."

"For what?"

"For leadership."

In my mind, the name Wrinkly wasn't at the bottom of the leadership list. It wasn't on the list at all. I was the last beaver in the colony that would ever be called upon to lead. Then the Spirit, knowing my thoughts, said:

"Those who lead must begin by serving others. It may have come from a sense of obligation on your part, but without a murmur or complaint, you've helped every beaver in this colony. That has been an important part of your healing and preparation for leadership."

"Leadership of what?"

"This colony, Brinkly That is your destiny."

I could hardly believe what I was hearing. "How can this be, I'm not a leader and don't want to be. Besides that, there's not a beaver in this colony that would follow me across the pond. We have the elders to show us the way," I insisted.

"The elders have served well," the Spirit continued "but in the future, the colony will need a leader who can guide them through dangers ahead. You may not feel like that leader, but I chose you for this purpose long before you were born. You see Brinkly, I specialize in using the weak to confound the mighty, the simple to shame those who think themselves wise and the humble to confuse the noble. In your weakness, I will give you My strength. In your dependence, I'll give you My wisdom and through your humility I will give you power to protect this colony. The elders have long been waiting for a strong and trustworthy leader to emerge."

"It should have been Gavi," I blurted.

"No Brinkly, you're wrong. It has always been you. Gavi understood that, and he fulfilled his purpose. Gavi knew My voice too, and he knew that I sent him to protect you. He was prepared to give his life, and he did. That was always his destiny. Be happy for him, he's with Me now."

I lowered my head and cried uncontrollably from the depths of my soul. How could anyone love so deeply?

"Brinkly," the Spirit continued, "Listen to me. Through that tragedy, humility and love have become pillars in your life. You've learned that the more you give of yourself in helping others, the more your love grows for those you help. Isn't that true?"

I couldn't speak, I just nodded my head yes.

"Without love, wisdom is wasted and without humility power is abused. In humbly serving the members of this colony, love has become a driving force in your life. Even the creatures of the forest have heard of your concern for others. When the time comes, they'll all look to you for leadership. And that leadership will flow from a heart of love, tempered by wisdom and administered with humility. So, don't worry what others might think, I've prepared their hearts. They see you much differently than you see yourself."

What could I say, I was stunned. I just sat quietly in the presence of the Spirit, and then He was gone."

Chapter 9

A Colony in Danger

By midsummer, the cool afternoon thunder showers had ceased. The suns relentless heat baked the forest while constant wind sucked every drop of moisture from the soil. Beneath the pine trees, the forest floor was brown and the vegetation brittle. The only green was the tall grass along the edges of the colony ponds. Older animals had seen this before. They knew what could happen without late summer rain.

One hot dry morning I glanced up, hoping to see a rain cloud. Something appeared to be falling from the sky. As it came closer I realized it was Regal; wings swept back to streamline his body, he was diving for the pond at top speed. Regal was our eyes in the sky, serving as an early warning system. Just when I thought he was going to crash into a lodge, he spread his wings full out and powerfully flapped to stop his descent, landing hard next to one of the elders. He sprang to his feet, "A fire has been started by campers. It's small now but it's racing up the mountain and the colony is directly in its path."

There was no time to waste! The elder had seen this before as a kit. His entire colony had been destroyed by a raging fire. He was one of the few who escaped with his life. He immediately called the entire colony together. "A fire is coming, we must evacuate immediately." Fear gripped their hearts, fire was the greatest threat they could ever face. The dry twisted branches which made the lodges impenetrable to predators provided no protection against fire. They were nothing more than kindling, consumed in moments by the fires veracious appetite. "If we leave now, we'll all be safe. Gather your families, we'll swim downstream together, the elder urged."

That's when I heard the Voice inside. It wasn't loud, but it was clear. "Brinkly, no one will die today, and not a single home will be lost. Here's what you must do." I listened and then yelled.

"We don't have to leave, I know what to do."

To my surprise, the elder stopped what he was doing and looked my direction. I could see the desperation in his eyes. "If you have an idea, Wrinkly, I'm all ears," he said.

"The fire is moving up from below. That can work to our advantage. The last fire destroyed the tall trees that once grew there. All that lies between the colony and this fire is thick grass and scrub oak. We can breach the dams in the upper two ponds, then direct the water to flood the open grass. While some are digging, others can fell the small scrub oaks along the edges of our colony and drag them downhill toward the coming fire. The fire will quickly burn through those oaks but be restricted to the dry grass as it moves further uphill. When it reaches the flooded areas, it will slow and die out. Our colony will be safe, and it will prevent the fire from spreading beyond our ponds into the forest. If it reaches those trees, it'll be unstoppable, and many lives will be lost."

Everyone waited, what would the elder say? "Okay Wrinkly, that's what we'll do. You're in charge, what should we do first?"

I didn't hesitate. It was as though something inside was guiding me, overtaking me. I heard myself directing the others with confidence and authority. "You, you and you," I said, as I pointed to the strongest and best diggers, "move to the highest ponds and breach the dam on the downhill side. The rest of you to the scrub oaks." Not once did I have to think about what to do next. I just knew.

By the time the dams were breached most of the scrub oak had been moved far from the staircase of ponds. The water was flooding through the thick dry grass along the entire length of the colony. We had done what we could, so we retreated to the tops of our lodges and nervously waited. Regal circled above in the smoky air. There was nothing he could do but watch and pray. I barked out one last instruction, "If the fire doesn't stop, dive for the bottom of the ponds." In my heart, I knew it wouldn't matter. No one, including me, could hold their breath long enough for the fire to pass us by. If my idea didn't work, the heat or the smoke would eventually get us all.

I hoped we had done enough. I hoped the voice in my head was not imagined. The longer we waited, the more doubt consumed my mind. I didn't want to die knowing I had been the cause of another tragedy, this one far worse than the first.

Then I heard one of the elders, "I can't see flames anymore."

Then another beaver further up, a little louder this time, "I can't either." Again, and again the reports echoed across the pond until finally they were drowned out by cheers and joyful slaps of broad tails on water. This little band of beavers had saved their colony and just maybe, the entire forest.

While the others cheered, I slipped unnoticed into the water and swam slowly to my lodge. I had never felt so good and so exhausted at the same time. Yet, sleep was not what I had in mind. I wanted to hear from the Spirit of the Forest. "Are you here?" I asked when I arrived. An unnecessary question of course, my lodge was filled with the aroma of roses.

"Yes, Brinky, I'm here."

"Please, tell me what just happened."

"You saved a colony."

"That's not what I'm asking. I wasn't myself today, something extraordinary happened."

"You're right Brinkly, I was speaking through your heart to your mind and you were listening. We were working together."

"So that's how this is supposed to work?"

"Yes, Brinkly, but are you aware of what else took place today?"

"I'm not sure what you mean."

"Like a guiding light in the darkness, your wisdom shined brightly before all. Those who once rejected you are ready to accept your leadership."

"Well, I don't feel ready," I replied.

"That's why I chose you Brinkly. I knew you would always look to me for guidance. Now, are you willing to take another leap of faith with Me?"

"Yes."

"There is one more thing you must do before you can lead the colony. I can't do it for you and it holds the key to receiving My supernatural power."

"I'm afraid to ask."

"Brinkly, I warn you, what you must do will force you to face your deepest fears and deal with the hatred you hold in your heart for the Black Ghost."

The very thought of the Black Ghost sent chills rippling through my body. For years, I had tried to bury those fears in the darkest closet of my mind, all the while allowing my hatred toward the Black Ghost to grow. Hate for him was the only feeling strong enough to suppress the awful guilt I felt for Gavi's death. And now, the Spirit of the Forest was shining a light into that dark closet, revealing my fear and hate.

"Brinkly, what I ask of you may seem impossible. If you should decide not to try I'll understand and love you no less. But I know you, and you can do this."

"What has the Black Ghost got to do with this," I stammered. "And what is this supernatural power you're talking about?"

"Patience, Brinkly, it will all be revealed soon. For now, just think about what I've said and remember, nothing is impossible with Me."

Chapter 10

Supernatural Encounter

For days, the words of the Spirit echoed in my mind. Then, late one evening, He returned.

"Brinkly, have you been thinking about what I said?"

I knew He wasn't really expecting an answer. It was clear that the time had come to learn of His request.

He continued, "Who do you think created the Black Ghost?"

What a question! Like a beaver's sharp teeth can peel the bark from a tree, exposing the core, this question exposed my deepest feelings. How should I answer? I believed the Spirit of the Forest created all life, but how could such an evil creature have been a part of that creation? "I don't know," I replied.

"Yes, you do," the Spirit insisted, "but you can't make sense of it. That's because My thoughts are higher than your thoughts, Brinkly. I alone possess all knowledge and understanding of life. Now, you must trust Me, and have faith."

After hearing those words, there was only one thing to say, "What would you have me do?"

Wrinkly's story was more than spellbinding. His words seemed to have a kind of power. Bump, who was usually as fidgety as a frog sitting on a sun baked rock, sat motionless. A rabbit could be seen lying next to a bobcat, unafraid. Tiny Fox was curled up against a log, his huge fury tail wrapped around a family of chipmunks to warm them. His words had affected all but one. And Wrinkly was the only one aware that he was lurking in the darkness of the woods.

"Shall I continue, Bump?" asked Wrinkly.

"Ya, PaPa, what happened next?"

The Spirit of the Forest asked me to join Him in the forest the next morning. He said He would meet me in a cave not far from where I had once tricked a bobcat. That location was forever etched in my memory.

Yet, I couldn't remember having seen a cave in that part of the forest. When I asked how I would find the cave, He said, "Listen to your heart. You know My voice."

As soon as the sun came up I was on the move. A few hours later I was standing on that very log. Back then, I felt like a conquering hero. But on this day, tears of regret and sadness trickled down my cheeks. Once free to roam, the bobcat was now living his life in captivity. I looked up, "I'm sorry," I said out loud. When the sorrow passed, I heard the voice of the Spirit.

"Follow that trail up the mountain. When you reach the top of the next rise, look up the hill to your right and you'll see a cave."

I had watched predators of all kinds use this trail to move quickly through the forest in search of prey. It was no place for a small defenseless beaver to tread. I stood quietly, staring up the trail, looking right and then left for any signs of movement. When I was sure it was safe, I jumped from the log. Slowly, I began walking as my heart raced and my body quivered. Then, like the chill of the morning slowly gives way to the warmth of the rising sun, the fear inside gave way to a peaceful calm. Somehow, I knew everything would be all right. When I reached the top of the rise, I stood tall and looked around. Just as the Voice had promised, I could see a cave in the distance. I left the trail and walked toward it.

About halfway there, I stopped. This was extraordinary. A strange glow was now emanating from the entrance. Like a bee is drawn to a pollen laden flower, the light was beckoning me to come. I rushed to the entrance. Most caves are dark and damp. When you step inside it feels like you're entering a cold black abyss. This was different. As I entered, the fragrance of roses filled my nostrils and a peace that passes all description or understanding flooded over me. The farther I ventured, the brighter the light became. At the end of the long winding tunnel, the cave opened into a brilliant cavern. The floor, the ceiling and the walls sparkled like snowflakes in the bright sunlight. Perfectly shaped crystals, some as large as a pine trees, were beaming rays of rainbow colored light in every direction. It was the most beautiful thing I had ever seen. And in the very center of the cavern was what looked like a ball of white fire. *Is this what heaven is like*? I wondered. The ball of light began floating toward me. As it moved it slowly morphed into a magnificent white bear, maybe twelve feet tall.

I dropped to the ground and covered my head. Not out of fear, but reverence. Then, He spoke.

"It's okay Brinkly," the Spirit said, "Stand and look at Me."

I knew that voice well and stood to my feet. With awe, I considered His beauty. His eyes, like a kaleidoscope of colors, changed from shades of blue to green and gold and back again. His white fur was luminescent, not reflecting the light, but creating it. Then He smiled, but there were no fangs. And when He reached out to me, I could see that His paw had no claws. When He touched my shoulder, love and compassion unlike anything I had ever known, flooded my soul.

"Brinkly, come sit next to me. I have a story to tell you," he instructed. "It's the story of the Black Ghost."

This was not a time for me to speak, just listen.

The Black Ghost

"The Black Ghost was born in the same spring as you Brinkly, and not far from the colony. His mother knew he was an extraordinary wolf the moment he arrived. His fur was not grey like the others in the pack, it was coal black and as smooth as silk. His eyes were steel blue; so piercing that he seemed able to look right through you. It was a sign of greatness in the world of wolves. His mother named him accordingly.

"Black Ghost is what I'll call him," she said. "One day he'll move through the forest like a black ghost with power and grace. He'll be a great hunter, nearly invisible to his prey. And he will lead our pack to rule the forest."

Not only was Black Ghost strikingly beautiful, he was the only pup born that spring. His father was the alpha male, the biggest and the strongest wolf of all. His mother was the matriarch and by far the best hunter. He became the center of attention and the hope for the future of the pack.

For the first few months of his life his mother never left his side. When he was old enough to leave the safety of the cave, his days were spent exploring and romping through the forest nearby. By summers end he was big and strong enough for his mother to return to the hunt. In the fall, he would be invited to follow the pack and learn how to hunt. Until then he was left alone in the den. He was still far too playful and clumsy to move undetected through the forest.

Early evening, Black Ghost could usually be found sound asleep near the entrance of the den. That's where he waited for his share of the spoils. He never thought much about his next meal, and, why should he? His mother had never failed to deliver dinner. But one cold fall evening, when Black Ghost awoke, expecting to find a hunk of fresh meat, his mother had not returned. In fact, there wasn't a single member of the pack to be seen. He let out a few howls expecting a response, but all he heard was the rustling of trees from the fall wind.

He had been warned to stay in the den until the pack returned, so there he paced and waited. One day, two days, three days passed with no sign of his family. What he couldn't know was that the entire wolf pack had been killed by trophy hunters. He was completely alone. And without the pack, the chances of Black Ghost surviving the winter were not good. No longer would he wake to an easy meal.

Black Ghost couldn't wait any longer. Hunger pangs grew stronger with every passing hour. He gathered the courage to take a few steps outside the den when a tree branch cracked in the wind and fell to the ground. He darted back in with his tail between his legs, shaking uncontrollably. When he calmed down the hunger pangs returned, stronger than before. Unsure, he ventured out again staying close to the den while looking for something, anything to eat. But no animal that might become dinner was foolish enough to venture close to a wolf's den.

Black Ghost was aware that another wolf pack lived in the valley over the distant ridge. Perhaps his family had joined them. He was afraid, but with hope fading for the return of his family, hunger drove him on. Carefully and quietly he moved through the forest, looking for signs of the pack. Days went by before he picked up their scent. Then, he tracked them by following his nose. At the edge of a tree line over-looking a grassy meadow, he stopped and scanned his surroundings. There they were, resting near the edge of a cliff on the other side of the meadow.

He carefully observed each wolf in the pack. Sadly, not a single member of his family was with them. He laid down and closed his eyes as tears dripped to the ground. From that moment on, he knew he would never see his family again. *This pack will have to become my new family,* thought Black Ghost. *Surely, they would welcome the most beautiful wolf in the forest.* That meant protection and a share of the food.

He stood to his feet and began walking, then trotting and finally running at full speed across the meadow and up the steep mountain to join them at the top. The pack of seven jumped to their feet and turned to face this strange wolf barreling toward them. He came to a sliding stop just in front of them. His excitement suddenly changed to absolute horror. Their heads were lowered with teeth showing and saliva foaming in the corners of their mouths. Their ears were flattened back against their head and the hair on their backs was standing straight up. He could feel the hate and saw it in their cold eyes.

They circled around him, cleverly blocking his only way of retreat. To his back was the edge of a steep cliff with a churning river far below. With every cautious step back, the pack took three toward him. They could smell his fear now, it was the odor that every animal releases when they know they're about to die. Then, without warning, they attacked. It was vicious and seemed to come from every direction. There was no escape. Black Ghost was defenseless against these powerful animals. He did the only thing he could. He jumped for the river. It was a leap that only an animal fighting for its life would dare make. The impact of hitting the water knocked his breath out. His ribs broke as he tumbled along the rocky bottom of the powerful river until it slowed into a calm eddy.

Injured and bloodied, he swam to shore and limped along the river's edge where he found a small cranny beneath a jagged rock. Shivering and weak, he crawled under and waited. If the pack discovered him the end would come quickly. But they never came. They must have thought he was killed by the fall. That's where he stayed for the next several days to lick his wounds and recover. He had learned a very painful lesson, the first of many and one he would never forget; no wolf pack ever accepts an outsider. There would be no friends in the forest for Black Ghost, not even among his own kind.

For weeks Black Ghost wandered, growing weaker by the day. His ribs were healing, but he was so thin that they could be seen through his once beautiful fur coat, now dull and dirty grey. The sockets of those piercing blue eyes were drawn and his eyes seemed lifeless. He was barely staying alive, living on dry grass, rotten berries and grub worms. That would not be enough to survive the harsh winter.

When the end seemed near, Black Ghost stumbled across a shallow creek that had not yet frozen over. With the little strength he had remaining, he decided to follow it downhill until he could go no farther. After hours of struggling he came to the end of the stream where it poured over the edge of a granite wall into a small pool. When he looked down, he could hardly believe his eyes. Was he hallucinating? He blinked and looked again. There, in a clear pool of water with nowhere to hide were dozens of fish. They had been trapped by the receding water in this shallow pond. A sudden surge of adrenaline rushed through his body. Half running, half stumbling, he circled around the cliff and down to the pond where he leapt in. Had the pond been any larger, the trout could have easily escaped his bite, but it wasn't, and he gorged himself. When he could eat no more, he curled up and laid down next to the pond. For the first time in weeks he had hope.

As Black Ghost lay there, his attention was drawn to a jagged boulder resting against the granite wall. Between them was what looked like the entrance to a cave. Fear again gripped him. Was this the den of a bear or mountain lion, or perhaps the home of another wolf pack? He stood to his feet and began moving toward the cave in slow motion, like a hunter stalking its prey, one quiet step at a time while keeping his body as low to the ground as possible. As he neared the entrance he couldn't detect the smell of a predator, just that of mice and chipmunks. The entrance was barely large enough for him to get through. But once inside he discovered a warm and dry cavern, the perfect den for a homeless wolf. It felt safe.

Each day Black Ghost went fishing and each day he grew stronger. Bitter cold winds were blowing now, and snow would soon blanket the forest. There were not enough fish to last the winter. He would have to learn to hunt on his own and fast.

A wolf pack has a huge advantage. They surround and pursue their prey until it's cornered or can run no longer. Then, they move in for the kill. Without the pack, Black Ghost realized he would have to learn a new way of hunting. That's when he remembered the prophetic words of his mother. "One day you'll move through the forest like a black ghost with power and grace, invisible to your prey."

That's it, he thought, *I'll become as stealthy as the mountain lion and a master of ambush.* At first, most attempts ended with him watching his intended target escape with ease. But little by little he perfected the skill. The escapes became fewer and meals were enjoyed more often. The advantage had shifted from the prey to the predator.

Over the next few years, Black Ghost grew into the most powerful and beautiful wolf in the forest, just as his mother had envisioned. But there were dark secrets buried deep inside his soul that even she could not have imagined. The pain of loneliness and rejection had turned his once soft heart into a heart of stone, as black as a starless night. The torment of fear had morphed into unrestrained hate and anger. And his skill as a hunter was no longer about survival. He had a more sinister objective in mind. He would become the most feared predator in the forest, the Black Ghost.

Forgiveness

Yes, Brinkly, I created Black Ghost, and I love him as much as I love you. What he's become was never in My plan. Perhaps now you can understand. If you are to lead this colony, you cannot harbor hate and unforgiveness in your heart. Eventually they will destroy you."

"How can I forgive the one who killed my best friend?

"I wasn't talking about Black Ghost, Brinkly. Forgiving the Ghost is easy, it's forgiving yourself that's difficult. And that can only take place when you first accept My forgiveness. One who has been forgiven much, is free to love much."

I bowed my head as my heart broke. The one I really hated was not the Ghost. And in that moment, I understood that I was forgiven. As I wept, the guilt that had weighed on my heart was lifted. The hate I had felt for myself and Black Ghost evaporated like mist in the warm sunlight. In some unexplainable miraculous way, I felt as though I had been reborn on the inside; old things had passed away and everything was new. Then, like a tsunami, joy flooded my heart. "Thank you, thank you, thank you," I whispered as I raised my head to look again into his kind eyes. His work complete, He had vanished. I sat for a while, waiting, hoping for His return. It wasn't to be. Soon, without his presence, the light of the cave grew dim, it was time to go home. But I was leaving with a new heart, overflowing with love and joy.

The setting sun caused the trees to cast their ghostly shadows, blanketing the trail in near total darkness. Yet, I felt no fear or need to hurry. I hummed as I walked, probably not the smartest thing to do if you want to avoid attracting attention. My mind was still gripped by the experience in the cave when I came face to face with a young mountain lion. He was standing in the middle of trail, surprised by my presence. I could only imagine his thoughts. I mean really, how often does a lions next meal come to him? I stopped and stared. The lion assumed the stance of a predator; eyes fixed, low to the ground, legs spring loaded for a lightning fast strike. He was waiting for me to trigger his genetic attack response by turning to run. Then, to my surprise, I smiled and said, "You're beautiful." I could hardly believe what I was saying. I was speaking, but the words didn't feel like they were mine. I could feel them coming from somewhere deep within, and they felt like they had power. When he heard, "You're beautiful," his ears perked up and he tilted his head to one side. Gradually, he relaxed. The look in his eyes changed from a deadly predator to what seemed like that of a friendly neighbor. Then, as casually as you can imagine, he strolled passed me, purring softly. I watched as he disappeared in the shadows.

Before this, I could not have imagined an event that would change my life more than the day I tried to outsmart Black Ghost. As awful as that was, it paled in comparison to the supernatural encounter of this day. I knew my life would never be the same.

"PaPa Winky," Bump blurted, "will you take me to that cave so I can meet Spirit of the Forest. I want to know His plan for my life."

"No, Bump," Brinkly said with a smile. "The Spirit will talk to you in His own time."

Growing in Power

Gavi was right, the Spirit of the Forest had a remarkable plan for Wrinkly's life. But one that could not be revealed until Wrinkly's misguided self-serving plans had failed. The Spirit didn't want Wrinkly to fail; but the white noise in his mind before Gavi's death, overpowered every rational thought. Insecurity, pride, and the cry for acceptance were like unrelenting screams, demanding attention.

After that awful day, all that Wrinkly wanted was to find a dark corner in his lodge and disappear. It was in that hopeless, dark, and quiet place that Wrinkly was finally willing to hear the Voice, and the Spirit rescued Him. He taught him that true leadership begins with a servants heart and a love for those you lead; that unconditional love is only possible when you can forgive others. And, most importantly, that forgiving others is impossible without first receiving and accepting forgiveness for your own mistakes. The plan for Wrinkly's life had to be built on a rock-solid foundation of proven character. If it were not, when the storms came, his leadership would collapse and bring the colony tumbling down with him.

The Spirit used a dangerous fire to empower Wrinkly and reveal his wisdom to the elders. From that day forward, whenever the colony faced a threat, the elders turned to Wrinkly for a solution. Somehow, in their hearts, they knew that his wisdom was originating from something or someone greater than himself. Recklessness had finally given way to wisdom and self-importance to humility.

It was in the winter, following his supernatural encounter with the Spirit that the elders asked Wrinkly to lead the colony. With his acceptance, little by little and day by day, the Spirit entrusted Wrinkly with more of His power. Over time it became so strong that some said you could see it when you looked into Wrinkly's eyes. Others said you could feel it when you were near him. But whether it was seen or felt, it was a power that no forest creature dared challenge—except one.

Chapter 11

Don't Be Afraid

Like a master story teller, Wrinkly took his family and friends on a journey of his life through time. Every beaver and forest creature was spellbound, living the story with him as it progressed. They had relaxed their guard and crowded in, inching and wiggling their way closer. Only Wrinkly was aware of what was still lurking in the shadows at the edge of the forest. When the story ended not one word had been spoken about the fate of Black Ghost.

Bump couldn't wait another second. "PaPa Winky," He blurted. "What happened to the Ghost?"

Wrinkly looked down at Bump and smiled. "You're about to see for yourself."

With that, the clear calm of that enchanted evening was transformed. Dark ominous clouds rolled in, obscuring the bright moon and brilliant stars. The air grew cold as a stiff breeze fashioned ripples into small white caps on what had been glassy calm waters. The wind came from the direction of the forest carrying with it a strange stench. A nervous bull elk lifted the end of his nose high in the air, attempting to identify the smell. He snorted, a sign that something was wrong. Alerted, the other animals stood to their feet. Heads turned, all eyes fixated on the edges of the forest. If an attack came, it would certainly come from there. Enchantment disappeared as a feeling of uneasiness, then fear, gripped every heart and mind.

Wrinkly spoke up. "Don't be afraid, we have a visitor. He has no interest in any of you, he comes for me."

"Is it the Spirit of the Forest?" Bump asked.

Wrinkly didn't answer.

Face to Face

From the dark of the forest a magnificent black creature emerged. Even from a distance in the dark, it was easy to see that this wolf was by far the largest to ever roam the forest. He paused and carefully surveyed his surroundings like a proud king waiting for his loyal subjects to pay honor on bended knee.

Nervous, the powerful muscles of the elk tensed and twitched, in anticipation of fleeing an attack. The deer were poised in a slightly crouched position. Like springs, their legs were ready to uncoil and bound for safety. Beavers moved near the waters edge while squirrels and chipmunks huddled near the entrance to their burrows. The birds sought safety in the branches of the tall tree near Regal's nest. Yet, not a single animal bolted. They unconsciously parted, backing away and leaving a clear path to the pond for Black Ghost.

As the Ghost moved closer, he no longer appeared so magnificent. His black fur was dirty and matted. Scars could be seen where patches of fur had been torn away, probably from battles with bears and lions. The whites of his eyes were yellow and blood shot. His jaw was slightly crooked, having been broken. His snarl and torn lip revealed a broken fang and missing teeth. Worst of all, he smelled of death. Years of hate and bitterness, like a cruel incurable cancer, were slowly and unrelentingly draining the life from their victim.

Not once did Black Ghost look to his left or right as he walked. He moved straight forward, eyes fixed on Wrinkly. He stopped at the edge of the pond, about ten feet from Wrinkly's lodge.

"You pathetic, little beaver," he said. "I've been listening to your touching story. And I've come to give it the proper ending. One in which an old wrinkled beaver begs for his life just before I end it."

Bump, who had been sitting directly in front of Wrinkly, stood to his feet. With a shaky voice he said, "You can't hurt PaPa Winky. I won't let you."

Black Ghost laughed, then his expression transformed from a distorted sneer to hate and anger. Eyes squinted, ears flat against his head, back hunched with the hair on the back of his neck straight up. A low menacing growl from deep in his throat filtered through exposed yellow fangs and chipped front teeth. Leaning back, he squatted down. Then in a demonstration of strength and power, he leapt from the shore to the lodge in one bound. With a single swipe of his paw Bump flew through the air. He landed hard near the shore, the air knocked from his lungs. He gasped for breath. Willow was shaking, holding tightly to Wrinkly. The Ghost showed no mercy, he grabbed her by the nape of the neck with his teeth and pulled her from Wrinkly's grip. Then slammed her to the ground and held her there with his huge paw on her throat. Saliva dripped from the corner of his mouth splatting on Willows beautiful fur coat as she struggled to breath. He lifted his head and looked directly into the eyes of Wrinkly.

Wrinkly stared back at the ghost. "Let her go!" It wasn't a request, it sounded and felt like the command of a general. "You're here for me, not a helpless kit."

Frozen in fear, every animal watched, unable to look away and certain that Willow's life was about to end horrifically. But to their amazement, Black Ghost slowly lifted his paw from her throat and pushed her to the side. She coughed, scrambled to her feet and dove for the water; then swam with all her might to the ponds edge where Bump was recovering. Wrinkly and the Ghost were now alone, face to face atop his lodge and only feet apart.

"You ridiculous little beaver," he said with a loud voice, so all would hear. "How do you feel now? Are you afraid, like you were the first time I stared down at you; your worthless meaningless life about to end? Or is it even more frightening now; knowing you're going to die while your so-called friends watch and do nothing? Have you forgotten what I told you while standing over Gavi's lifeless body? "Your time will come, and it has." Then, leaning forward, he whispered so only Wrinkly could hear, "Who will save you now?"

The Power of Love

Wrinkly's answer unnerved the Ghost. "It's you who needs saving, not me."

The Ghost backed up and laughed. It was time to end this once and for all. "I'll make this quick," he declared.

Wrinkly knew that beneath that evil look was a desperate fearful animal longing to be set free. Compassion filled Wrinkly's heart. "I love you Ghost, and so does the Spirit of the Forest," he said. The other animals could not believe what they were hearing. How could Wrinkly possibly love the very one who had killed his best friend?

Black Ghost recoiled as if he had been struck a blow. "No one loves me, and I love no one," he yelled at the top of his lungs.

"You're wrong," Wrinkly replied. Then he moved close to the Ghost, reached out his paw and stroked his crooked jaw. Black Ghost started shaking, his legs grew weak. Unable to support his own weight, he dropped to the ground.

"What's happening to me?"

"This is your opportunity," said Wrinkly, "for your heart of stone to be transformed into a heart of flesh. Remember the love you felt for your mother and the love she gave to you? That still resides deep in your black heart. It's like a seed that can spring forth into something beautiful if you'll allow it."

The Ghost's breathing became shallow and labored. He knew exactly what was happening. He had witnessed it more times than he could remember. These gasps for air were the signs of a dying animal. He rolled over on his side and lay on the ground unable to lift his head. Wrinkly knelt next to him and whispered, "You're forgiven, all you need do is accept it."

For the first time in many years tears filled the Ghost's eyes. "Thank You," he whispered, his voice so weak that only Wrinkly could hear. Then he closed his eyes and seemed to breath his last. No one watching dared say a word.

Wrinkly began to lovingly stoke the head of Black Ghost. As he did, something miraculous happened. The fur of the Black Ghost changed. It started at the tip of his nose then moved over his body. It was transforming from black to pearl white, almost luminescent. When it reached the tip of his tail, the Ghost took a deep breath.

The creatures around the pond stood motionless, looking more like statues than living animals. None said a word. The Ghost stood to his feet, silhouetted against the deep blue, moon lit sky. His jaw was no longer crooked, his steel blue eyes, now set in sockets of pearl white fur were crystal clear as he gazed into the heavens.

The Ghost then turned to Wrinkly. "You and I have some place to be, don't we?"

"Yes, we do," replied Wrinkly.

The Ghost knelt and Wrinkly climbed on his back.

Only Bump had the courage to say anything. "PaPa, where are you going?"

"The Ghost and I are going to the top of Pikes Peak, I've always wanted to see the sunrise from there."

The rest of the animals stared in disbelief as the Ghost carried Wrinkly up the mountain. Regal took flight and followed from above.

It wasn't long before they arrived atop the peak, just before sunrise. Waiting for them was the Spirit of the Forest as Wrinkly had imagined him, in the form of a beautiful white bear. And next to him, with a giant smile on his face, stood his best friend, Gavi. For the first time in his life Wrinkly watched the sun light up the valley of his home below. While he did, his fur too changed to a beautiful pearl white, not a wrinkle to be found. When he finally noticed, he looked up to Regal.

"Tell everyone in the colony I love them and tell Bump I'm expecting wonderful things from him."

And then they were gone.

About the Author

 Some kids call him "Grandpa Jimmy," probably because he's old. He's a little like the character, Wrinkly Brinkly. His face is wrinkled and kind of furry. His five grandsons think his beard is cool while his only granddaughter says it's scratchy.

Grandpa Jimmy loves to write stories for kids. If you ask him to go hiking or biking or even snow skiing, he would say yes. But you might have to slow down a little, or maybe a lot, so he could keep up. If you ask him to tell you a story, you might find yourself turning off the TV or setting your game aside, at least for a little while.

Grandpa Jimmy and his wife of fifty years live in Monument, Colorado, which is nestled against the towering Rocky Mountains, not far from the Air Force Academy. These rugged mountains are the setting for many of his stories.

Jim & Shirley Ertel

Follow the adventures of five sixth grade friends and a mutt called Bandit. They live in the small town of Buena Vista, tucked away in the rugged mountains of Colorado. Tall mountains covered in dense forest, steep canyons and raging rivers are their playground, or at least they were.

And their clubhouse, well, let's just say that the tree house in Ben's back yard lost its appeal. They have laid claim to a hangar built in the 1930s, the ghostly home of a forgotten old airplane.

According to Grandpa Jimmy, the owner of the hangar, if that remarkable plane could talk, it would tell a thousand stories of adventures and intrigue. He often says, with a smile and a wink, "This old bird is magical."

The planes battered aluminum skin has long since lost its shine and one engine is missing. It obviously can't be flown. Yet, when the gang steps inside and closes the door, it magically transports them into a world filled with adventures. One that only they believe exists.

Kids Helping Kids

You can help! When you order a book from Grandpa Jimmy, part of the purchase price is used to help these children. The purchase of one book will provide two children in need with a healthy lunch.

That's right, you can help boys and girls just like you. The only difference is they live in the poorest communities in places like Nicaragua and Mexico. Most live in shanties, have one set of clothes and often go without shoes. Attending school feels like a miracle to them.

Ambassadors to the Nations is an organization that builds schools in countries and places where no schools exist. At these schools, children enjoy the warm, nourishing lunches that kids like you provide. For many, it's their only meal of the day.

Ambassadors to the Nations also gives the children school supplies, uniforms and one pair of tennis shoes each year. This may not seem like much to those of us who live in America, but to them it's everything.

Thanks for helping,
Grandpa Jimmy

If you enjoyed *Wrinkly Brinkly* or any of the
Hangar One online series,
I would love to hear from you.

You can reach me at:

Grandpa Jimmy
P.O. Box 2111
Monument, CO 80132
Website: mygrandpajimmy.com
Email: mygrandpajimmy@gmail.com